CW01099893

Sovereign

Sovereign Invalid

Alan Cunningham

Dostoyevsky Wannabe Experiment
An Imprint of Dostoyevsky Wannabe

First Published in 2018
by Dostoyevsky Wannabe Experimental
All rights reserved
© Alan Cunningham

Dostoyevsky Wannabe Experimental is an imprint of Dostoyevsky
Wannabe publishing.

Preliminary work on this text was completed during a 2013 residency
at the Zentrum für Kunst und Urbanistik in Berlin, funded by the Arts
Council of Northern Ireland.

Cover Design by Gary Prendergast
dostoyevskywannabe.com

ISBN-13: 978-1721879496
ISBN-10: 1721879498

A few years ago I overheard the phrase 'Sovereign Invalid' being uttered by an economist, or politician – or someone of that ilk – during an interview on a TV programme and it sparked something in my mind. He was referring, I think, to certain member states of the EU but I can't remember whether he was being critical or complimentary. I've tried to source that interview so I can credit him and clarify what his stance was, but I can't find it – or, maybe, as I now think, the whole thing was instead a dream I once had…but then perhaps this amorphousness of origin – and position – is in keeping with the spirit and form of the following text.

"There might also be a language in whose use the soul of words played no part."

Ludwig Wittgenstein, *Philosophical Investigations*.

SUCCESS, leading to failure

1.

You stared across an almost empty carriage – there was someone sitting on the other side.

They stared into the distance of the window opposite.

You looked at their body and then at their face. They took out a phone. They looked at the screen, their face impassive. Then their lips stretched and you saw their teeth.

Laughing, you thought.

Beautiful, you then thought, still staring at them and hoping they might stare back.

You realised, then, that you had it hidden under the bag that lay upon your lap.

You thought about taking it out and putting it on display for them – and anyone else – to see.

You left it where it was.

•

{ *What else could you have done?* }

•

They started to shake their head at the message they found displayed on their phone and continued to laugh – but now a little more wickedly than before. Then they began the process of reply. Once finished, they placed the phone down on the crotch of their jeans and laid their hand flat on their leg.

•

They closed their eyes.

•

The persistent nature of your stare had an effect, however. They sensed something, something impossible to ignore. They roused themself up, looked to their left, then to their right and then, to your very real surprise, they found your eyes. Their eyes, you thought, were the color of a favorite leather belt of yours, bought during a trip to Genoa.

{ *This — I think you know — is just too much* }

They didn't waver, though. They held your gaze. A familiar panic then ruined your body and you thought — *Why? Why now?* — about more laughter, about a possible future scene of misfortune and intricate sadness.

Not possible, you thought — *inevitable.*

You lowered your eyes and your head and then looked, a little shamefully, out through the window opposite.

•

{ *You know nothing of other people* }

{ *And what is it they've ever done to you?* }

•

You thought, then,

> {*You imagine*}

about... well,

> {*You shall call them*}

...*them*, as you walked out of Angel station and on to Upper Street — about the role of your story, together, in the inevitable descent back to: shame.

•

> {*There is always the presence of another*}

•

They had told you that they loved you, but y⸢
about the – *well, what is it? What? Absence?*
the – *no, a* – lack.

> { *There is always the something not talked about* }

> { *There is always knowledge of the incorrect word* }

> { *There is always the word of judgment* }

> { *There is always the lack* }

Well, you had talked about it, in round-a-bout ways, but you always felt that you had buried so many of your real feelings on the matter that all that was left to speak about was a kind of residue of what you felt and thought, a kind of choking dust.

When, at certain points during your life, that dust had momentarily drifted away, it revealed the presence of what you now thought of – after having seen some during a holiday in Egypt – as antique columns built only with silent anger, half buried and extending meters down into what you supposed could only be your soul.

> { *This, oh once again, is just too much* }

The columns had been there for what felt like centuries and supported the weight of something neither visible nor understandable – some form of sorrow.

None of them had ever really liked it when the dust occasionally drifted off.

Neither anger nor sorrow had very much appeal to them.

•

Or maybe the columns were supporting that other thing, often times too horrible to even think about at all.

•

ʝu'd felt it more than they had ever realised, but, then, you never wanted to make a big deal about it.

You knew, *of course*, from talks with friends and family, that

"Yes…well…"

{*Someone always says*}

{*Trace of guilt discernible in the eye*}

"no one can ever fully accept the body…can they?"

•

But isn't there some way we're to be judged?
  Isn't it o.k. to feel – then – somehow cheated?

> {*Strange for you to think like this*}

> {*It is all that you can imagine*}

•

And yeah, you thought regardless – *it really*

> {*EMPHASIS*}

> {*OH NOW COMPLETELY PERSONAL TO ME*}

– *it really, well yeah… it really, truly is.*

•

And then, the habitual rebuttal – *get over yourself.*

•

{So many more, oh much worse off than you}

•

It was this type of thinking that had stopped you from talking honestly with them about any of it.

You saw yourself as different but you didn't want to talk about it at all and, *anyway, are you*?

You just wanted, as everyone so often advised – and always, always felt – to *just try to fit in and get on with it.*

{*You doubt you wanted this at all*}

{*You are trying to be new, and to be good*}

•

But then, then, every so often…

•

A memory of a feeling – a memory of what you now called youth, equating happiness with it.

•

{For isn't happiness youth?}

•

You began to recall long forgotten moments that you had spent with them.

Moments, contact and, somewhat more embarrassingly, certain forgotten feelings that had resulted from such moments and such touch.

•

Most awkward of your recollections – you gently rested your head upon the window of the Overground train that you had boarded and thought, feeling the cold, hard glass against your forehead, about lifting it up again and bringing it down hard – was a remembrance that you had become obsessed with them – *about another human being? Oh Jesus Christ* – in the earlier days of your coming together.

You remembered taking some kind of new and extraordinary joy

{*Impossible to define*}

in your train journeys home from work, knowledgeable that they would be present in their flat upon arrival, doing the things that they routinely did there. You remembered thinking about them when you were not with them, thinking about when you would see them again, and what you would do together when you were reconnected.

{*That first feeling*}

You remembered how you started to form a picture of your life – the shape that it would take – around them, while they, you thought, and sensibly, only continued with their own as they had always meant to do.

•

So you thought now.

•

You wanted to stop all recollections but closing your eyes offered no assistance.

You started to worry about the current motion of your life.

{ *You would be glad of the change* }

All this memory threatened the rhythm that you had set.

{ *There was no discernible rhythm* }

You felt a brief panic in your body.

•

{ *You felt alive* }

•

You opened your eyes but found that you couldn't look out at the streets any more, nor at any of the shops, bars and cafés you could see along the route.

Why have you come back to this part of town?

You knew the reason for your presence there – it was an accident of circumstance, a necessity imposed by work – but you asked yourself again:

Why have you allowed yourself to forget all of this? Surely you couldn't have thought it wouldn't matter?

You stood up, ready to get off at your stop, the next one. Some characteristic of routine in this movement caused you to think about how long it had been since you had lived in the area, and you thought, then, of all the buses and trains you had, during a period of your life, taken from this stop. This thought calmed your panic, somehow. It made you think that perhaps your current memories were prompted simply by not having been there for a while.

You had not been in so long.

You had searched for a connection between the present and your past and had found a joyous and forgotten one, and that had overwhelmed you. The train stopped and you hurried off of it once the doors opened. You left the station, looked around and attempted to see the street as it was now, not as you remembered it.

{*Not unimaginable*}

•

You moved your body forward, toward your meeting.

•

But you could not think only of your meeting.

{ *Who can think only of meetings?* }

You wanted to ignore the memories now remembered, prompted by being there again, but you could not.

{ *Who can ignore such things?* }

You thought, instead, and indulgently, of how you had felt when you had been invited into their apartment, two buildings over from where you stood. You looked at the butchers, located beside the main door, and recalled the feeling of physical joy you had once felt upon realising that you would always have a landmark to remember where they lived.

{ *Who would reject indulgence?* }

You remembered their loose Brazilian character, their skin browned by years of sun exposure.

•

{ *And who would reject the westward facing sun?* }

•

You also remembered their laugh, *yes*, and how they had made gunpowder tea that first evening, talking all the while with a childish delight about a long forgotten television show that was of no particular interest to you. You had felt important to them. You had felt that you mattered and that your presence made things better.

{ *It was no doubt very different* }

•

I had nothing to feel good about, you thought.
I liked feeling wanted — but they were just alone.

•

Perhaps.

•

The sight of the butcher's shop, its anglicity so peculiar on the high street, made you think then of specific instances where you had felt that unexpected and unexplainable joy in their company.

{*Almost impossible to quantify*}

You remembered how once, after waking up to find them feeling unwell, they had announced their intention of getting out of bed to prepare a lemon drink – how you had asked them to remain where they were and had indeed offered to prepare it for them before you left their flat for your own work.

{*You had wanted to just leave*}

"No", they had insisted, rousing themself up and laughing, "I'm very particular about hot toddies when I'm sick."

{*You are sure they did not say toddies*}

There had been a loving future together implied in such intimacy and informality of language.

{*This you think true, no matter what words were used*}

So you had thought at that time. It was a lack of any connection now with the person you had been then that made you tired of such memories.

Tired and a little sad.

•

{*This you think true, no matter how you felt*}

•

You looked through the window of the bus during your ret.. journey and saw a girl standing on the pavement, crying, and finding – so you thought – some comfort in a boy's embrace.

Take that comfort.

The girl kissed her boy, again and again, and cried as she placed her hands upon his chest.

He held her, and said nothing.

•

"You're looking young", you then heard a man say to a woman.

"Oh, that's just what I wanted to hear", the woman replied, laughing, as she sat down right beside him.

•

Sovereign Invalid

Remember.

•

You remembered a train journey to Edinburgh with them and how they'd had a sweet tooth the whole way there. You remembered how you'd tried to persuade them to not eat too much chocolate.

"That *Kit Kat* is winking at me again", they'd said, quietly, every time the tea trolley had gone past.

You'd looked at them with comic exasperation and they had smiled.

•

Remember.

•

You remembered a video that you had seen online the week before, an advert made by a London gallery in an attempt to get people to sign up to a destruction workshop run by an artist. This, you remembered, an artist well known for having once destroyed all the possessions he had – by that point in his life – somewhat imperiously accumulated.

"Bring an object you want to destroy to the gallery", he'd said in the video, smiling.

"I brought my teaching planning book from last year, and a radio", one of ladies in the video had said, reflecting on her session, smiling also, giggling almost, and you had thought *how so particularly easy it is to destroy such common things.*

•

You thought, then,

> {*If you can continue with the story*}

– sorry, if you would, perhaps, be so kind as to do so now – about their flat, and about the things that they had had in it. You were envious of the ability others so often had – so it appeared to you – of being able to fill their apartments with things that had meaning for them, things which comforted them and which brought them joy.

  You had no such ability.

> {*You had lost it*}

You found comfort only in the things of others, if in things at all. Your greatest pleasure was always the delight you felt in being in the apartments and bedrooms of others, others you thought totally unlike you, people who had an apparent stability in their life and whose decoration and furniture reflected an ability to stay, to be somewhat comforted by things familiar.

> {*You wanted to steal a life*}

> {*It was the only way you thought that you could have one*}

•

You thought of that moment when you had visited them in their new flat, after you had made the decision to leave – and of how you had often wished you had simply stayed there that long night.

{ *This you rarely thought*}

It had been fear that drove you out – fear and the impatience of youth, which so often cannot permit of any difficulty.

{ *Though some do say their youth does make them patient*}

•

If only I had waited I would still be there now and not thinking about it, and them, constantly.
  But how, you thought then, disturbed and frightened by the clarity

{*And bad poetry*}

of your thinking, *can a vision of the past equal one happy future?*

•

You walked, as you always did, toward the next bus stop but before you reached it you felt the strap of your bag – slung over your left shoulder – fall and touch your elbow. You felt the bag start to drop from your shoulder. You looked down at your right hand and thought of how you now wanted to hold the prawn noodle salad box – bought in *Sainsbury's* not five minutes previous – in another hand, but then you felt conscious – as never before – of realising something else, something you had attempted to ignore for far too long.

Frail from this reality, you stopped walking, kneeled down and placed the box of food upon the pavement.

{ *This was last week* }

You placed the salad box down upon the dirty London street and then you stood and rearranged the straps around your very weakened shoulder.

{ *This was last week* }

You saw a man get interrupted by another as they passed each other. Their arms went up – *go to my side, go past*, both said, impatiently, without words – and you looked, then, at their eyes. They looked dissuaded by the presence of other bodies on the street and, *yes,* you thought, as you awoke – *we can be interrupted by another.*

{ *This is today* }

Have not only I the precious gift of matter?
Is my body not the only one?

•

Sovereign Invalid

You are again disturbed by this lapse into what you can only think of as

> { *This is bad poetry* }

•

Then, later, a woman got onto the bus that you had taken and, after entering, looked up at the CCTV monitor. She wiped beneath her eyes. She did not look content. Another woman, wearing, you thought, a *newly purchased dress*, walked past the bus as it stopped at traffic lights. She, too, looked at her reflection in a shop window – fixed her dress – and then moved on, moving somewhat differently than before.

You continued to look out the window.

Yet another woman walked by and pivoted round strangers and you thought, then, as you watched her *there is good will in her body and even some left over for the others who surround it.*

•

{ *There is always room for grace* }

•

Jesus but the sight of men wearing cufflinks makes me nauseous.

•

Two women stood outside Liverpool Street station, dressed in tight, revealing one-piece suits of the kind worn in strip clubs. They handed out flyers and other things to passing men and a sign nearby indicated that they were advertising a Gentlemen's Club. You peered out of the bus window, engrossed. You saw things that excited and disgusted you.

Calves, the promise of a buttock.

Cufflinks.

You looked down from the bus and you wanted to look, to look at flesh and people. The girls glanced around the street, unbothered by admirers for a moment, and you thought then that if they looked up and caught your eye you would feel something odd yet resolutely possible – a shame for having looked at them. *Why?*

I want to look.

And what is it I am looking at exactly?

Something I have seen a thousand times before.

•

I still…I want to look.

•

You looked, then, at what remained.
No.
Not what remains.
What does not exist.
What did not continue to grow.

•

You held up your right hand also and compared the two extremities, ignoring the stare of a stranger. Instead of a thumb you had something impossible to describe with only a word.

•

{ *Try anyway* }

{ *That is what you are here for* }

•

Sovereign Invalid

It was

> {*Then*}

the same size as a hook

> {*Hook*}

that one might hang a coat

> {*Coat*}

from, it was made of dark flesh and it was part of your body.
You thought you saw, for a moment, the beginnings of your life.
Then, you corrected yourself, as always.
More like the never seen.
The never seen life.
Not meant for eyes.

•

Following, in a neat row, from the stuck beginnings of a thumb were four incomplete fingers.

No.

Not fingers.

Not even that.

Four collections of dark matter.

Matter before fingers.

Matter with remnants of whatever it is that becomes, in time, what we know to be a nail.

•

{ *There is a lesson here* }

{ *And yet, you find – you loathe them* }

•

People moved forward.

•

You walked with a deliberate slowness between them. You toyed with the Oyster card in your trouser pocket. You turned a corner and emerged from the tunnel of advertisements into a large atrium. Two escalators led people up toward the exits and the street and one carried them down toward the trains. You took your place on the right-hand side of the middle escalator and looked upwards.

You looked at the faces of the people who were descending. You looked at the bodies of the people who were ascending, not being able to see their faces.

You saw – two powerful thighs upon two strong calves, all connected to two substantial buttocks.

You were entranced.

The thought of being able to feel that flesh began to incubate you from the stench of the Underground. Intoxicated, you kept looking. Arriving at the exit, you moved quickly forward, past the other passengers, to see if you could see to what kind of face it all belonged.

It was a woman.

•

You were surprised, then, by your ability to think this fact somehow incongruous with what you'd seen whilst traveling upwards on the slowly moving escalator.

•

Then, near Holborn, while walking to work the next morning, you saw a man sleeping on the pavement outside a *Pret a Manger* cafe.

You looked closely at him then looked around to see if others were looking at him as you were. You looked through the window of the *Waitrose* supermarket opposite and noticed that a woman was paying for her items at an electronic checkout. The woman raised her eyes, briefly, and looked out at the street, at the man sleeping on it.

She looks disgusted by the sight of him, you thought, and then, you thought, looking away from them both *and why was I looking at her, and no longer at him?*

And why was I looking at him?

•

Later, holding your phone between your teeth in order to free your right hand – so you could discard of an empty crisp packet – you wondered, once again, about the looks of those who worked and walked the streets.

The looks of the others around you, and those looks of your own.

•

Look.

•

You started to look, finally, and the people at whom you looked in return looked surprised, as if you had reminded them what their eyes were for, as if they needed reminding.

Look.

I'm here, you thought, walking, thinking they all could hear you. You wondered how this had happened. How had they – and you – forgotten?

You looked at towers that rose from streets of London, known and unknown, finished and in progress. Had the general form of *up* resulted from male experience? What if women had been the first builders, what if they had had to develop in that way, long ago?

As if they hadn't.

You imagined dwellings and offices placed deep into the ground, windows out of which light shone toward opposite windows across frightening chasms, windows that had to be looked down upon, houses that now favored cover and enclosure instead of elevation, subtlety over pride.

•

Probably would have been all just the same.

•

Alan Cunningham

At the reception of the office where your next appointment was, you introduced yourself to the receptionist.

"Hi", you said and then you waited, politely, for some kind of reaction.

You waited to see whether the receptionist would stop looking at the computer monitor in front of her.

"What's your name?", you said, putting your right arm on top of the wooden barrier that was placed between you, surprised to then see shock.

•

At the foot of a *Royal Bank of Scotland* building in Southwark, you contemplated engaging in unspecific acts of terror directed against financial institutions, acts immediately reconsidered after first the thought of death and second realisation that even if successful the financial system might collapse and that you would somehow suffer.

•

You didn't want to suffer.

•

Alan Cunningham

On the steps that lead up to London Bridge a man was sat.
He asked you for change and you said
"No",
deliberately ignoring the feel of a pound coin in your pocket.
"S'all right", he smiled back at you and you saw that both his
eyes were very red.
"It's, what, no, it's, it's the…"
He paused, unable to quickly form the word he wanted and
you predicted ignorance, inability.
"…most common answer at the moment, s'all right."
"Sorry", you said, turning then to take another look at him.

•

You walked on.

•

Sovereign Invalid

You waited in another office, sweltering and quiet.

•

"Did you see that thing on telly last night?"

"The woman who had 15?"

"She weren't on benefits or anything."

"But 15. And she wants another one."

"Where'd they get the money?"

"I think it's cruel."

"They went on holiday, did y'see that?"

"With her parents too."

"How'd they afford that?"

"Me and Mike can't hardly get away for a week these days."

"I think it's cruel myself."

"What'd you have for lunch?"

You saw a large photo of two boys, hung upon the wall.

"Sponge cake. I was thinking about you when I was eating it."

"Sponge cake. Hmmm. Haven't had one of those in ages. Used to be my Saturday treat, you know."

"I'll bring you one back tomorrow, if you like."

"No. No, don't do that."

"Why not?"

"If I eat one, Lucy – I can't stop."

•

Was it work that had changed your understanding of words –
and of people?

They had become only literal; thus now incapable of change.

It is as other things that they can redeem, you thought – *it is with
change that respite is offered*.

If you could change them, maybe…but words – and people –
had come to mean what they meant. Your job – the thing you
did for all your money – demanded this of you.

You felt unable to resist. You found yourself without a world.

You're lucky, you thought, *you're lucky, lucky…*

You're lucky if the words you use – or people met – mean
perfectly what you think maybe just once within a lifetime. If
an accident of circumstance occurs. And how often will others
understand you even then?

{*Even less than once*}

How have I survived at all?, you thought.
How is it that I've not yet gone quite mad?

•

You continued to talk English – and meet people – nonetheless.
The job – did you ever find out what it was, in fact? – well, it did
demand such things of you.

But you had travelled to other countries, of course you had –
had even lived in a few of them for a time. You understood the
impact strange architecture and new scents had on the ability of
a body to relax – or maybe even defend – itself.

•

Forgiving all of that, you now felt uncertain in London. The possibility of damage frightened you.

You saw threats everywhere.

{ There are other views on this of course}

Threats: holding cups of coffee in your mouth with only teeth for purpose of opening closed doors, scratching interiors of cloth with a protuberance uncommon, purchasing coats and jackets to contain unsightly, fearing coming summer months and demands for flesh, preparing coins for quite efficient payment.

It was now a world much more prone to control and not necessarily given over to impulse.

•

{ There are other views on this}

{ Look around, at this new city}

{ Look now at yourself, for goodness sake}

•

Then

    { Then: }

"I'm going to the other city."

"What, for the weekend? D'ya get a cheap flight? Should be nice. You been before, ain't ya?"

"No. Not for the weekend. I'm moving there. I'm going to go and live there."

"The other city? D'you speak the language, then? Why you wanna do that?"

"I like it there, oh yes. I want to get out of London for a while, I need a break. I've been before, yes yes. I do not speak the language, no, no no. That doesn't seem to matter, no, not much. I will not need to understand it all, oh no, oh no, I'm sure I won't – oh no. It's cheap, of course, oh yes – it's very, very cheap. I will not need that much to just get by. I'm sure I will of course receive some work out there, oh yes, oh yes – I'm sure, I'm sure. I'm sure that I will like it all, oh yes."

•

Oh always yes.

•

You thought, then, about your mother and your father, how they'd become, at some point in their lives, people who travelled, and who had travelled.

People who could not remain.

•

You thought about how your parents had travelled away from their places and countries of birth, how they had both hated and enjoyed it, how you, now, were once again traveling away from what you'd come to call a home.

Your mother had phoned you two days previous from Portugal. She had reminded you that she was returning to Ireland. You thought about what she always said to you before she flew somewhere, *be nice to me, I might not come back from this, these planes, these planes, my God.*

You thought about what she always said when you now spent time together, *I'm tired, now — I'm tired — I don't have long before I croak, you know.*

•

You decided to take a train to the other city.

•

You did not know why, other than that you had become somewhat afraid of flying. You were aware that this concern was without much basis, *but from now on,* you declared to yourself as you paid for the ticket, on-line, *I wanna indulge my eccentricities, and not feel like I need to hide them.*

You took a bus to King's Cross station.

You got on the train.

The train was full.

•

At Cologne, waiting for your connection, you walked outside of the station – which you turned to then look back at and admire – and glanced up at the cathedral, confused and delighted.

{*It frightened you*}

The night train from Cologne was made up of carriages of various provenance – Czech, Polish, German – and you were disappointed, although somehow not surprised, by the uncomfortable nature of your appointed seat.

•

You arrived in the other city during darkness.

•

You took a train to another station, got out of the carriage, walked up the stairs and over a bridge that crossed a river – *the sun will soon come up*, you thought – and took note of a new lack of concern within yourself regarding the presence of other people – people, on the streets, just doing nothing, admiring sunrise.

You decided to delay your arrival at the hostel. You walked in the darkness, turning slowly to day, then stopped at a small bakery. You bought a tea and sat outside, and could only wonder at the city.

Blackness started to turn blue, animals began to communicate with each other and human voices were heard around you as the city, and part of the world, woke up.

Look at how beautiful it is, you thought.

At the table opposite you, a young man drank occasionally from a red plastic cup and spun, repeatedly, a coin upon the tabletop. The city slowly changed as light continued to emerge with more power and presented – comprehensible form.

Nobody paid any attention to you – *everyone,* you thought, *has their own concern on their mind and not that of any other.*

•

You were falling out of love.

•

And the next day, after waking, you watched him and you let him struggle.

•

{ *You like to watch the struggle* }

•

You waited patiently as he made his way down the stairs, his unresponsive feet tapping against each metal pole of the handrail as he pulled himself down and along. As he approached the bottom of the staircase, people sitting in the foyer saw him and rose up from their seats. They looked worried.

{*You like it when they look worried*}

You were happy to wait the interminable length it took for him to descend the few last steps.

{*You like interminable length*}

It was the waiting itself that caused you happiness.

{*You like waiting*}

You looked at his arms as they shook with the strain of manoeuvring his own bulk down to the bottom of the stairs. You admired their movement and their strength.

{*And you like strength, fool that you are*}

"I've got to get to the centre of town for two", he kept repeating, in English, to the person who carried his wheelchair alongside him, as if an explanation was necessary for his descent.
He was sweating.

•

The lifts had not been working that same morning, you then recalled.

•

Later that same day, you sat behind a girl from Colombia and watched what she looked at on her computer screen. She was looking at a magazine called *Spotter*. You found yourself wanting to look at all the things this girl looked at on her computer on a computer of your own, but you did not have one with you. You wanted to sit behind her and mimic her every action, her every selection, so that your screen matched, exactly, that of the Colombian girl.

Every time she clicked into a new website you would do the same, yes, or…

•

Or so it was you thought.

•

You had come to the hostel as a stranger, frightened by the necessary proximity to other people. Ten days later, as you prepared to leave, as you stepped up a ladder to close the one, tiny window of the room that you had slept in you felt the potential of missing even it, this small, unhappy room of your short residence, bedroom to four people.

Anything can become home if you let it, you thought and then, learning, you modified the thought slightly – *if there is no other choice.*

The next day, after moving into your new apartment – the details of how you obtained this apartment in the other city, the money involved, the paperwork photocopied, the use of the Internet to obtain addresses and locations, the Internet cafés given custom, the beauty of the interior, shabbiness of exterior, the pleasantries exchanged with neighbors, all of this is of no interest here, of course – you sat down, and – well let's not quibble now – you *ate*.

•

You ate honey and butter – real butter – smeared onto *McVities* digestive biscuits. You hadn't eaten such biscuits, or butter – or even honey – for years and here you were, eating – *what is the word for such things? Constructions?* – made from all three, each aspect heaped on top of the other. You chewed and tasted and swallowed, often without thought, tasting only sweetness and salt and feeling the dry paste of the biscuity construction in your mouth.

Then you thought – *Yes.*

You remembered something, and that something was what made the stuff within your mouth – the combination of that stuff – so distinctive, beyond any specific taste of each part or beyond hunger. That something made you pause and eat and think. And made you keep eating. You remembered your grandfather, and his small kitchen, and eating digestive biscuits, butter and some strange type of Canadian honey on those days when your mother had been too busy to pick you up from school.

•

The next day, though, you shopped.

•

You had avoided buying new clothes before going to the other city, even though you had recently seen many things in London that you had been tempted to buy – a leather jacket, new trainers, some jeans.

Wait, you'd thought to yourself, *you'll find more unusual things once you get to the other city, things that nobody else will have when you decide to return to London.*

Now, in the other city, wandering the streets around the centre in search of stores, you regretted your previous indecision. Looking into window displays and through them you saw nothing you liked and, even more so, felt pangs of regret for the comfortable and comforting style of London.

The thought of your body in any of the clothes you saw was painful to you now, although in the wake of that pain, you let yourself realise, without much difficulty, was also a trace of some strange and new sensation of pleasure.

•

2.

You walked past a bar on the way back to your apartment. Large windows provided all who passed by with complete exposure to the actions of those inside.

You walked a little more slowly than usual as you passed, afraid of stopping completely but still curious enough to try to see what, exactly, the people who frequented the place looked like. There were tables placed alongside the windows and these were inhabited by young, dishevelled, attractive men with beards and glasses and women who smoked cigarettes and drank beer from large bottles.

Something had always prevented you from stopping when you'd walked past it before – stopping, walking up to the door, pulling it back and stepping inside to see what came of it all.

You paused and turned – walked back to the closed door – and then, belligerent, you opened and you entered.

•

You could not say with any clarity why you went in there that night. Perhaps you had become more comfortable in the other city.

You felt content with yourself that day.

You felt content within your body.

•

{ *Be good, now* }

{ *Be gentle* }

{ *Forceful* }

{ *Oh hell – whatever is preferred* }

•

{An admission, first, before you continue, proof, then, that you consider it somewhat sinful – you have only interest in beauty}

•

{Although here's the other thing with awful beauty, now remembered – in time it gets forgotten, it has to always be recalled}

•

Strange and unwarranted words interrupted your thoughts as you opened the door.
Erotic.
Functional.

•

Look.

•

You disregarded the words and decided to sit at a stool by the bar.

•

Behind the bar stood a tall, underweight white bartender, perhaps, you thought, in their late twenties. They raised their eyes up from looking down at whatever it was they had been looking at just prior to your arrival. Then they lifted their chin up and down quickly in recognition of the appearance of you, of your position at the bar and – most of all – your recognisable desire to order.

They did not say anything.

"A whiskey", you said – a little loudly.

"One whisky" they confirmed, and then, after turning, grandiloquently, and indicating with a wave of their right arm the numerous varieties of both whiskey and whisky that were on offer, they turned back around to face you and they smiled.

{ *This is just too much* }

"Your choice."

They nodded.

"Ice?"

"No ice."

"Single? Double?"

"Double."

They nodded again.

•

Aquarius, read a very bad tattoo on their left forearm.

•

You allowed your eyes to follow the actions of the bartender as they went about the business of preparing your drink, but you were not paying much attention – if, indeed, any at all – to what they were doing. You were more interested in what was happening, currently unseen by you, behind you. You wanted to turn – slowly, gradually – around and look at what was happening in the bar, but you knew that you would not be able to do so with the confidence necessary until you had a drink in your hand.

You waited.

You had glanced at the people who were still drinking, smoking and talking behind you after you had opened the door and walked inside, but the real look you had made then had been toward the bar – to identify an available seat,

> {*Untrue*}

to attempt to establish a connection with the bartender,

> {*Irrelevant*}

and, most importantly, to indicate – however false or true it was was not of any importance – that you just did not care who else was in the bar that night.

•

> {*Inaccurate*}

•

Then, you sensed a look – directed, so you thought, towards you.

•

You could not explain how it was that you had sensed it, nor, even, whether you had done so with any real accuracy, but you knew, somehow – *yes*, you whispered slowly to yourself, *yes yes, I know* – that someone was looking at you – that someone had been looking at you, in fact, since you had first walked in.

You felt you looked ridiculous in the clothes that you had decided to wear out. You had wanted to drink, to unwind, to be amongst people – you had not necessarily been desirous to be with them. You had chosen your clothes accordingly. Now, thinking that you were being looked at, and reacting to that – wanting and not wanting to – you wanted, perhaps, the look to last. You did not want to take off your overcoat.

{*Everything else you wore exposed your skin*}

•

You took a sip of your whiskey. You held the glass tightly in your hand as you swallowed. Then, stepping down a little from the stool so that your feet touched the floor, but leaving your ass perched on the edge of the seat, you moved, slowly, to the right.

•

Give them the look, someone else then happened – or indeed decided – to partly think.

The look.

They like the look, initially, because it is an attempt at illustrating some power, whereas it admits of no power, or, rather, another power, one of gentle subtlety and of beauty – their own.

They first constructed this sentence in their mind, using words they had learned over the duration of their short life to give some logic to their experience.

Satisfied, they then lifted up their pencil and they opened up their notebook, then they wrote the sentence down.

They took their time while writing, careful to replicate the thought exactly as they had somewhat partly thought it. They were aware of some necessity for it to be remembered exactly as it had been first partly constructed in their mind.

Then, finished, they put their pen down, and they looked up and they looked at you.

•

Sovereign Invalid

You had turned around.

•

You gave, as you looked out at the bar crowd from the comfort and elevation of your bar stool, a certain type of gaze to them all, new and frightening in its coolness. You had not prepared, nor been prepared for, such ability. If you caught the eye of someone, whether man or woman, you held their eye. There was no discomfort felt by you, nor, you thought, by the other. Instead you felt there was a mutual understanding between yourself and those you looked at. Not that many of them were looking at you – only a few did so and the rest continued with their conversations. Between yourself and those that did look back, however, there was an unspoken agreement, you thought – *things can be done to them and by you, to you, by them, if they were willing as you were willing*. If they indicated their willingness further. For the gaze was already a show of willingness, of a sort – an understanding of where things could yet go.

None of those that held your gaze, however, were in any way attractive to you.

You got ready to turn back around and face the bar again. As you started to turn, however, someone who had been writing throughout put their pen down, looked up and looked at you.

You stopped.

You held their gaze, but were not prepared for – or had, perhaps, always been awaiting – them, looking at you, like that.

•

Appropriate, you thought to yourself, although if asked you could not have said why you thought so, the music that had been playing – guitar charged asinine pop – changing to become a series of repetitive, pulse stimulating beats played out over the plaintive, faintly spoken words of what you imagined to be a young and blond English boy.

You held the gaze of your admirer with one equally lustful and accepting, although not quite so convinced of the character of its giver. You smiled at your observer, as they smiled at theirs.

They understood – rightly – your smile and look as an invitation to join you and placed their pen and notebook in a small holdall by their feet. You relaxed – they understood something of what was meant by your look. You worried that you did not yet fully understand their look or your own. You felt that you had been encouraged by something, however, and put worry to the back of your mind. You understood, looking at them stand up, pick up their drink and bag and walk toward you, that this meeting might lead to nothing, everything, or something traumatic. You understood that and you looked at their eyes with that knowledge in your mind, and they continued to walk toward you and looked back.

•

{ *Quiet now please* }

{ *Impossible task* }

•

You were less fearful than before, you almost thought, the potential for rejection based on what was seen having diminished. Something in the manner of their approach had made it so. *Anyway*, you thought – *I've still got my coat on. Nothing might happen yet.* They arrived at the bar, dropped their holdall to the ground and took the seat beside you. You turned the stool around to face the bar. They looked away from you, momentarily, to catch the eye of the bartender, and your sense of comfort left you for a second. You thought they had played a cruel joke on you and cursed your stupid arrogance. But, their task completed, they looked back at you – at your eyes, still looking at theirs.

Nothing was said between you.

"Yeah?" asked the bartender.

"Same again?" they asked you.

"Why not?" you said – smiling, as they were smiling.

"Same again."

"What were you writing about just then?", you asked.

"Ha. That. Well. I was writing about looking. About how I should…" – and here they paused and smiled – "about how I should, well… look. How I should look at you."

"You're a writer?"

"Not really. I write. Just like you saw. That's all. I write, sometimes, to think. To clear my mind."

"And you were thinking about how to look at me?"

"Yes", they said, taking out some money from their pocket.

They passed it to the bartender.

"Why did you need to think about it? Why not just look?"

"Like now?", they said, smiling and they sipped, gently, at their drink.

"What's that you're drinking?" you said, holding their gaze, stifling a desire to smile, as they were smiling.

"Rum and Coke. Would you like to try some?"

They pushed the glass toward you.

"No. No thanks."

"So – you didn't answer. Am I just looking now?"

You smiled.

"That depends. What's looking? And what's just looking?"

There was an ease to their manner that made them somewhat

tolerable.

.

Of this they sadly knew.

.

"Well, I gotta go."
  "I'll go with you. I only came out for a couple."

•

You stood up – and then you left the bar together.

•

And at some point during the walk after, you, or they, pulled you, or them, into the entrance doorway of the apartment building and pulled up, or lifted, the jumper, or shirt that they or you were wearing and looked with admiration and with function and with lust at the mass of others torso.

Did you or they really want to fuck them, or you, to have sex, make love, to feel a pleasure swell up from the center of some gravity as a confluence of matter then occurred, to feel a pleasure from that?

No.

You or they wanted to see them or you feel pleasure in another way, a type of pleasure uncommon in everyday matters, a kind of animal squeal of joy that they or you were responsible for.

It was the responsibility for action and for joy that excited.

{ *Immeasurable joy* }

That, or you or they did want to be right fucked, to turn all moderation off and genuflect upon a bed or floor of matter.

•

and you or they also wanted to see them or you look upon that pleaszzure, and be pleassszzzured b tht.

•

"There's something I want to put in you", they later – though once again quite very gently – said.

"No, please, I don't really want you to put anything in me just right now."

"But I just want to. Don't worry. Natural, like."

They laughed.

"No, no, apologies, that's my mistake – not *quite* as nature has itself – I'm sure – intended."

•

They laughed again.

•

Something in this phrase excited you, though. You wanted to be fucked – you wanted to fuck – in a way, like they had said, intended – or not intended – by all nature.

•

You wanted to feel natural – and unnatural. You wanted to be touched and to be held.

•

You wanted to feel free to then receive: all different kinds of rough and gentle touch.

•

"Can I move yet?"

"I'd prefer it if you didn't – not just yet. No, in fact I don't want you moving at all. This isn't going to be about pleasure. I want you to perform for me, all right? That's what I want; it's what I think I want. What do you think? What do you want?"

•

That they thought you an instrument suitable for performance excited you.

You wanted to be such an instrument – or, rather, to be thought of as being such.

•

You could see, then, that they were attracted to deficiency, or, rather, emboldened by it, and thus allowed to feel alive. You were happy to be an instrument for their pleasure, being not quite ready enough to know how, or even why, to take your own.

{ *This will change* }

{ *It must* }

You lay back on the brown leather sofa and took some comfort in the weight and substance of your body. You could see how much they liked it, how much they were ignoring what remained.

{ *Oh, let them ignore it* }

You were ignoring it also, and you focused, instead, on the elements within and around you that were still powerful and not at all frightening.

{ *Let us not speak of it* }

You spoke, without words, of the power of each other and recognised the limit of what was being said in your movement and your peace.

{ *Let us not mention it* }

•

Of this they did not mind.

•

They had taken off their jeans and their briefs and held, proudly, a thing in their hand.

They walked over to where you lay and, kneeling on the sofa, patted the head of the thing onto your lips – an introduction. You were perfectly still and had retained the cool, welcoming gaze that you had fostered in the bar. They looked at the thing. You worried about not being good enough for them and about being too good. You wanted to be perfectly good.

{*It is doubtful that you worried*}

They wanted you to be good.

{*It is safe to now assume*}

They knew that to be an indication of something. Everything else they were not convinced by, but that, that goodness, like their goodness, told them something, told them they were doing something right, or, at least, something was happening or had happened to provoke a response within you. They liked the absence of what just happened to be missing, they decided, although to look at what remained disgusted them slightly.

{*Think it a novelty*}

{*Think of it not at all*}

They thought about that absence, instead, and constructed another sentence in their mind, although they would later forget it. It was the lack of something they had, in another, that brought them joy – that, and the fact that you were sufficiently good and look pained and that thing was now inside you.

They placed their lips down upon yours and you kissed, messily, the taste of each other's saliva a necessary and successful combinant for your activity.

The taste of this, each one then thought.

•

This.

•

{ *New words not now needed* }

{ *No, not really necessary at all* }

After sex, they quickly left.

•

They then texted someone from whose attachment they had separated after one had told the other (in somewhat – no, in *very* – very different terms) – *one night whilst out drunk with friends and you were away for work I ended the night by having sex with someone else*:

"*Just had sex. Their body is more beautiful than yours has ever been. They are younger than you.*"

•

Two days later you noticed they had sent you a request.

The day after that you realised you had immediately accepted it.

•

3.

Ok then – you wrote –
   imagine

> {*Imagine*}

you're standing

> {*We meet*}

in a doorway

> {*It's late*}

on a summer night

> {*The weather's disappointing*}

and are waiting

> {*And you've been waiting*}

for me

> {*For me*}

•

suddenly
  – you continued –
  you touch

       {We touch}

your lips on my shoulder

       {Without words}

you smile

       {You look good}

and look down the street

       {You like me}

and ask me to stand in the door way

       {We kiss}

and lean against the wall

       {Ask how each is}

you lift up my shirt

       {Take arms}

get down on your knees…

       {And walk toward a bar}

              •

!!! you're leaving it there?!
  thought you'd gone and wanted to check

> *{You seem shy}*

How could I leave?

> *{You ask me again how I am}*

  Well ok... you spread my legs

> *{And what I would like to drink}*

then slowly

> *{And you walk to the bar and order}*

with a finger, trace a line

> *{You want to hear me speak}*

  from my ankle

> *{About my dreams and aspirations}*

to thigh

> *{About where I grew up}*

take your ass in my hand

> *{The experiences of my life}*

lift it up

> *{The tragedy}*

and lick from calf to thigh

Sovereign Invalid

{*And the pleasure*}

•

you're warm

> {*You care for me*}

you're making me warm

> {*You want to look after me*}

that makes me smile

> {*You want me to be yours*}

i play with my tongue on your chest

> {*Your possession*}

suck slowly on your skin

> {*To direct*}

bury my face between your legs

> {*As you request*}

feel your legs buckle

> {*Owned*}

a hand on your ankle

> {*But admired*}

holding you there

> {*Walked with, outside*}

to

Sovereign Invalid

    {My arm}

be

    {In your arm}

continued...

    {The pleasure}

what!!

    {Of your breath}

...in the best possible way

    {The pleasure}

well,

    {Of your smile}

as long as it makes you happy

    {The simplicity}

hope you're not doing anything bad

    {Of your talk}

not yet. but I will

    {About television shows}

my nipples are hard

    {Online magazines}

tight under my shirt

> *{ The sweet gifs you send me}*

pinch them for me

> *{ On Facebook}*

hard

> *{Meaning nothing to you}*

yes

> *{But nonetheless brightening}*

now

> *{My day}*

what are you wearing

> *{So that I think of you}*

jeans. and boots

> *{And picture your lips}*

a jumper

> *{As you sleep}*

undo the button of your jeans

> *{And your eyes}*

and pull

Sovereign Invalid

{*As you wake*}

yes?
the zipper down

•

You did as they had asked.

•

You were happy that they were not right there – happy that another could provoke your body and your mind – but also happy that they were not there any longer – could not be – to touch.

•

They were also happy that they were no longer where it was – that *there*.

•

The next day, then, having begun the very important process of forgetting all of that, you pushed some money – a euro coin, let's say, then two twenty cent pieces – into a ticket machine and you waited. You played with the ring you wore on the index finger of your right hand. It was a plain silver band, once gifted by a friend.

A ticket dropped into the cavity in the right-hand corner of the device and the noise it had been making stopped. You pulled the paper out and had it stamped with date and time by a validation machine.

You walked toward the stairs.

You looked at the ring again.

Nice, was all that you could faintly think.

You smiled at how pathetic that thought was but also at how the ring embellished – properly – your lifeless skin. You stuffed the ticket into your coat pocket and looked, once more, at your hand as you took it back out.

•

The other hand you kept within its pocket.

•

The left arm of your coat was too long

> {*Can you not see?*}

and, you thought, when visible only made what was considered missing to be much more unavoidable.

•

You rarely walked in public with both arms out and by your side. You favoured coats with deep, wide pockets. You never felt it right to simply alter the length of any clothes you bought – you preferred to leave them as they were

> {*For what were they, those purchased, borrowed clothes, to someone just like you?*}

– to adapt, instead, your body to the world that had been created in spite of and around you.

•

Or was it that you simply rued the world?

•

Opposite the platform, then, plastered along the wall that ran the full length of the tracks, was a large picture of a pretty woman with long, strait, blond hair.

She, too, had a ring on her index finger, a big golden mess of one that was topped with an attractive – though almost ridiculously large – pink diamond. Her hand was placed upon her cheek and the whole scene, you thought after some real consideration, had been photographed and edited so that the ring shone with a beauty that was difficult to ignore.

You looked at the platform monitor.

{1 minute}

You heard the familiar noise of air being sucked out of and pushed along the tunnel. You stepped back and looked again at the picture of the woman, at the grace of her body and the way her right hand rested delicately against her cheek.

Her other hand was placed against her hip.

The train emerged from the tunnel.

You tried to look at the picture again, but before you could focus on any detail of it the train rushed past your line of sight and started to slow down in preparation for the delivery, and loading on, of all the other passengers.

•

You walked toward a set of doors, then stood to the left of them so that once opened those on board could easily get off. You took your hand out of your pocket and looked, again, at your skin and the ring located around your middle finger.

The train doors opened – you continued to look down.

Those who had been waiting on the platform – those who also wanted to get onto the train – started to crowd around behind and then in front of you, disrupting, in typical fashion, what could otherwise have been a peaceful exchange of passengers.

You did not move.

You waited.

You waited until the last person who wanted to had left the train and then you walked slowly on and stood by the windows of the closed doors. You placed your hand around a pole for support and, looking absent-mindedly through the window, you saw, once more – though closer, now – the body and the hands of the pretty lady in the picture.

The train began to fill up.

You ignored the presence of those around you and looked, instead, at the glittering stone that dominated the picture. You could feel their shoulders against your own, all those people, you could feel their warmth and – *yes, oh yes* – their awful, awful breath. You looked away from the picture and then once more at your hand, coiled around the soothing metal pole.

The driver announced that the doors were closing and then all those who were standing around you readied themselves – as best they thought they could – for the inevitable acceleration of the train.

•

In the carriage you had just entered you saw – then recognised – a boy you knew, a boy who lived in London.

He was partly dressed in drag, a predilection somewhat known to you.

He saw you too – called out your name.

You smiled at him.

He and his friends danced over to you, drunk, and tinny music played from a small speaker one of them was barely carrying. They danced around you, then, and they asked you to also dance. You did so, quite embarrassed. Your friend, though – he smiled throughout. One of his party took an earring and a wig out of a bag, placed the wig on head, fixed it, hooked the earring into ear.

Your friend swayed with the movement of the train, his eyes completely closed.

•

The placing of the earring on the boy as he pretends to dance, you thought, imagining it as a sentence in a book – and you realised it disturbed you.

"It's me", though, the boy then said, smiling – and he took your hand in his.

It didn't matter that you knew who he now was.

The placing of the earring on the boy as he pretends to dance – this thought, your thinking of it still disturbed you.

•

And then, a very great time distant later – and some concurrent distance from train stations – you heard a lot of pretty words being slowly and, you found you thought, quite sensitively sung.

•

You had pushed a café door wide open and had walked right through the arch, right through inside.

•

You unravelled a scarf from around your neck and then took off your hat.

•

You stood and glanced at the people sitting and standing around you and at the small stage far off to the right. There was someone there, on stage, lit and still singing one of the many lines you had just heard upon your entrance. You kept looking at them as you took off your coat. It looked like they were about to take the song in another direction entirely and then you felt a tap upon your shoulder.

You turned around.

"Hey."

A friend held a half empty beer bottle in their left hand and a hand rolled cigarette in their right.

They smiled at you.

You listened instead to the word *beauty* being sung, then realised you had not replied to them.

"Hey" you said, slowly – "When did you get here? I didn't see you when I came in."

"Not long. An hour or two ago."

"Who's that?", you asked – and then you nodded at the stage.

"The singer?"

"Yeah."

"I don't think you want any of that", they said, laughing.

•

You smiled.

•

They finished their performance, walked off the tiny stage and sat down. They took out a cigarette. It was difficult not to look at them. You walked over and pointed at an empty seat, nearby.

"This free?"

•

They looked at you and nodded, then they lit their cigarette.

•

Returning with a beer, you could not then stop looking at their lips, at what they were saying with them, how they laughed and how, when they laughed, they appeared much younger than they no doubt really were, how they were chewing bright green bubble gum.

If asked today, you would struggle to remember much of anything you said that night.

"Another?" was one part of the conversation you remembered.

"Yes" was their reply.

•

{ *Oh always yes* }

•

You drank another drink.

You looked at their eyes and felt a strange exhausting comfort.

•

Your body shook and you thought the following while not listening to what was being said and while looking, instead, at their lips and thinking your only available option was to kiss them – *they are beautiful, sublime, a person of extraordinary power and strength, a person of selflessness, a person without ego, a person without desire, a person without constraint, the freest, the best, the most reliable, the most considerate, the most beautiful, the most non-violent, the most musical, the most sensual, the one who will remember, the one who will remember, the one who will sacrifice, the one who loves best, the one who saves, the one who cleans, the one who works, who understands, who listens, who cares, who likes, who enjoys, who is honest, faithful, considerate, temperate, self-knowing, soft, not hard, the most delicious, gregarious, insidious, dangerous, rambunctious and most delightful.*

•

You wanted to fuck.

•

> {*List continues*}
>
> {*Becomes untruthful*}

•

You felt a delirious comfort in their presence, intuited that they, other, felt the same, knew it to be perhaps only a chemical reaction or aftermath of psychological damage but enjoyed it anyway, knowing it to be something.

•

Sovereign Invalid

{ Oh always something }

•

Then, being a thinker, you continued to imagine the possible implications of it all, pausing only to think again about what kissing them might feel like, looking at their lips and considering them once again quite beautiful lips, the finest ever seen, what holding them within your arms might feel like, imagining it to feel…

•

"I like you", you said – from almost nothing.
"I want to kiss you."
They smiled.
"Later" was all they said.

•

Sovereign Invalid

First you had another drink.

•

Then, you left the bar in search of others.

•

Some other things were said, of course – in your slow, unsatisfying walk to drunkenness.

•

Each order for another shot of whiskey or vodka in each new-found bar was, to give example – though perhaps it only seemed that way to you – a secret communication from you to them and back again but not really understood by either even then.

Something was being said, yes, you found you thought – but what?

•

Eventually, somewhat happily, you realized – you thought you realized – that it was something about a respective need to not withdraw; a need, instead, to touch.

•

You had not expected to feel like this.

•

You had not expected to think such thoughts and what is more, with much less hesitancy surrounding them.

•

You wanted, simply, to touch.

•

When you had first thought – and then instantly blurted out as your walk continued – "we need to get drunk" – you had done so, so you had believed, with only an expectation of a fuck.

You knew drunkenness to be the standard preparation for such an act but had forgotten how long it had been since you had had the need to remember such information.

You had not wondered, although you did so later, soberly, at the strangeness of remembrance of that long forgotten fact.

•

The meaning of what was happening filtering through the noise of every bar, you saw that all of it – the shots, the promise of just one more, the search for another, another, another – had been preparation for something quite different than what you had first imagined.

You saw that it had been preparation for an innocent but still raw act, for the frightening simplicity of what now felt only inevitable – your somewhat desperate, somewhat joyful need to not recoil from one another.

•

Drunkenness had thus been necessary, you realised late into the night, not because you had wanted to fuck, although that was probably going to happen. No, it had been needed because you'd had no useful guide as to how to respond to the feeling that was distracting you both.

It had been necessary for the same reason that sobriety had become much more the norm for you since you had been in the other city, because the world – your world – had once been turned completely inside out.

•

"Let's watch a film", they later said.

"What do you want to watch?"

"I don't know yet. Come back to mine though. We can watch it on my projector."

•

You walked up the stairs, then, later, always later – slowly, patiently. *One step at a time*, you thought.

•

One –
step –
at –
a –
time.

•

You wanted to observe them.

•

They were bound, currently, by streamlined skinny jeans, vertical seams flowing up and down the curves of their cheeks and thighs and leading the eye that chose to look, finally, to the small of their back or of their leg.

•

I want my mouth around that, you thought.
I want to bury my whole face right there.

•

And should I touch them, then?
No.
They can touch me if they want.

•

But I – for some unknown, particular reason – no, I will not touch them.

•

You sat, instead, and awkwardly, on the narrow blue sofa that ran along the length of the right-hand side of the room. They sat beside you, their knees folded – almost completely – into the cavity of their chest. They watched the movie in silence, for the most part, laughing at points where it seemed most appropriate to do so. Occasionally they would let out a gasp of what sounded like astonishment, momentarily unaware, you thought, that it was a movie you were watching and not a scene from real life.

I can't, you thought, the drunkenness receding – *I can't, I can't. I just don't want to.*

•

But you continued to watch the movie, for you did not want to leave.

•

And then, the movie ended.

•

The light from the projector faded and you were returned to near darkness, no other lights in the room having been turned on. You had remained in your respective positions for the length of the film, but, over the course of the film, one outer thigh had come to touch and then gently rest upon another without anything being said or acknowledged. There had been no recoil. If asked, neither of you would have even remembered it ever happening.

"You can sleep here, you know – if you want."

•

You were certain they were tired – but you did not want to leave.

•

"Stop", you then realised you had heard – but this, oh so much later.

•

"Stop", you heard again – and now a little louder.

"What? What's wrong?"

"Not much. No, nothing in fact. I just want you to do something for me, though."

"What?"

And then – a pause:

•

"Stand up. I mean, get off the bed. Stand over there."

They pointed at the middle of the room.

"Why?"

"Just try it. Don't worry, please. I promise – everything will be ok."

•

You pulled the duvet back. You placed your feet down upon the floor. Then you stood up and walked straight forward.

"Stop", they said.

You stopped.

"Now turn around."

You did so.

They looked at you.

"You have a body – did you know that?"

•

You said nothing – but then you looked into their eyes.

•

"Stay where you are", they said, now laughing very, very gently.
"I'm coming towards you. Don't move."
They stopped – and then they pointed at the floor once again.
"Don't you ever leave *that* place."

•

{Such useful knowledge}

{Not quite enough}

{More will be needed}

•

{But tell me please – oh why?}

•

4.

This, then, was that place – your place within the other city:

Where metal, painted soft green, trundled slowly and gracefully, where haulage carriages were lifted, where gas was stored, green lights burned painlessly atop temples built to honor grain, rivers flowed, nature recaptured the city.

•

Serbian restaurants, deserted, gathered mould unto their leatherbound bosom.

•

Weddings occurred on the street, by passers gasped and listened.

A man told his friend to open a coffee house within his small photography shop.

Once opened, nobody came, so the friend returned day after day, establishing residency to keep his friend from regretting the decision, subsequently uninviting passersby who thought, *there are people already in there, it's so small a space, another would be pushing it, keep walking.*

•

But it was not the city.

•

On the edge of the city – it was not the city – where haulage came and went, attraction was close, goods were close, the city was close, sophistication – close, company – close and loneliness was yes of course so very close.

Fidelity – close, faithlessness – close, where ships came and went, where produce sat, was shipped to and from and sold, where some people lived but not many, and some others came there too but went away again. Art was close and coffee was close and beer and sex and so too were quiet streets with nothing happening on them, streets you walked along and felt lonely on but not really, no, perhaps it was like this in NYC and London and maybe even Ireland too?

•

{There is always the Internet to guide the way}

•

You had moved to that other city after being in cities and countries, other cities, where nothing had happened but buildings were full of light and people, the shops were there but closed then and mothers reclined on chairs in well-lit living rooms, watching television while daughters threaded their eyebrows for the next day when they would return, fully loved, to that old city.

•

You thought about how you had loved – and where you had been.

You had loved with too much care.

You're so careful, they'd once said.

{ *A lover's rebuke* }

•

But careful, you'd always thought, *for surely some good reason.*

•

And thus – regardless eyes – and some months later – you then thought:
Please don't touch me.
Just don't.

·

Don't even try to talk.

·

You fought an instinctive reaction to say these words – you did not want to upset them.

You did not want them to think that you no longer found them quite attractive.

You knew they would not like to be thought of as being such. You were not even sure you felt the way you thought, but the proximity of body was having an adverse effect. It had been some months since you had first met. Somehow, you knew what their reaction would be if the words were duly uttered.

•

{And would your reaction not then be the same?}

•

You did not want to upset the comfort and pleasure each took from the fact of the other.

•

You did not want to upset, rather, the relationship that allowed such comfort and such pleasure.

•

Alan Cunningham

You could not replace your body, however, even though you now ignored how it retreated from what was usually a connection you enjoyed.

•

Another moved towards you, then – they had to touch you.

They had to touch your face in a way understood by one – by both?

In a way, at least, remembered.

•

You moved away, slightly.

You did not want to be touched. Your body did not.

Something in you refused it now.

•

You wanted to say words that gave some recognition to this fact, but you did not want it to be you that said it to them – and not you to any other.

•

{You work for nothing}

{You value nothing}

{You expect everything}

•

{You have no faith}

•

Do you understand what I understand?, you thought – yet did not say.
This is about us.
You and I.
I need to know that you understand what I understand.
You need to know this too.
I understand.

•

{You have no faith}

•

Weeks later, though, inhaling a smell from an unfamiliar t-shirt you had found in a chest of drawers, it was not their smell, it was not even the smell of a name, but it was a smell, a memory of something. Outside the sun moved such that it disappeared from view, the lack of cloud in the sky and the bright glare of that great ball bringing a memory of joy up from within you, a memory of

.

And now I want to touch again, you thought – *or is it to be touched?*

•

It would be an act of idiocy – you knew that it would jeopardise so much – but you thought again of how… no, no, not true… you thought instead of nothing, nothing noteworthy at all.

•

You thought, instead, of nothing and you sat and felt alone.

•

Sovereign Invalid

They took me into their apartment.
They gave me money.
They rubbed my back, feet, hand, hair and temples. They bought me
lunch often and they took me to the cinema.
I have nothing — no property of my own, no savings, nor pretty clothes.
They go away for a weekend. I lie in their bed and find I cannot sleep.

•

{ It is not some kind of touch you want, then}

{ But it is something — something else}

•

But you continued to refuse familiar – found it now well…
much too real – and so continued to fight the familiarity caused
by days and nights of sleep and contact; touch.

This bothered you, when you recalled your appetite for touch
and your despair when you were kept from it. It bothered you
when you felt that appetite again in relation to a newer, less
familiar body.

Am I only my desires?, you thought.
Even when able to think?

•

But it was of course so clear that you understood the way familiarity crept in, and boredom. You understood the techniques that were suggested to combat all of that. And yet still you looked at others and thought about touching them delicately, exploring the strength and tension of their bodies and having them explore you, and more importantly, all your weakness.

•

You thought these things – you did, you really did.

They excited and they frightened you, in some equal, awful measure.

•

Wanting the body, then –

{*It is not the body that you want*}

•

Standing in the room of the gym that contained the mixed showers and remembering how the last time you'd been there someone had entered after you'd left the shower and had started – so you saw, out of the corner of your eye – to undress in preparation for a game.

{*How to ignore such things*}

•

You had wanted to touch.

{*How to ignore touch*}

•

You had wanted to stand and to watch them undress and then: to touch.

•

The idea that that could happen and that you could both then walk away, neither offended nor obligated to the other in any kind of way had excited you in a manner not previously experienced.

You and I, you had thought.

{*How to ignore another*}

You and I.

{*How to have faith*}

A picture.

{*How to avoid beauty*}

A photograph.

•

{*And how to avoid your death*}

•

And the next night, you watched them on stage, used to their performance now, no longer entranced by it, no longer thinking of that first feeling of joy. You thought about weakness and, then, for some reason, writing. Sometimes, all you wanted was to be strong and to have a beautiful body – to be whole.

> {*Is that not what is prized then – to be whole?*}

With that, you thought, *I could be very happy.*

•

And then you thought *but surely not forever.*

•

I get it, you then thought, shopping once more the next appointed day, standing by the railings of a square in the centre of that other city, feeling a faint yet tangible regret concerning your forthcoming absence from the place – looking at the accumulation of fabrics, colours, cuts, and styles and at the complexity of it all, fashion, at the suggestions offered by cloth – or words or images; or even also anything – of what people believed in – and believed themselves to be.

•

{*Their great obscene identity*}

•

Looking down at it, now exposed, you were amazed by its existence.

•

You thought, for a second, that you had some understanding – a glimpse – of what it was, or what it could be – and then came the choice, thankfully – but then words failed you – or didn't – and, *no,* you thought, again, *perhaps – perhaps? – I do not have any understanding at all.*

Not at all as you so often imagine it to be, was all you could come up with and you felt dissatisfied by the blandness of that.

•

You saw where you were going, and you were not necessarily afraid, although you were, as ever,

•

There is a bird on the end of my arm, you then thought, overtaken by your own imagination, as you looked down at the shape − *a bird where my left hand should be.*
I can see its beak.

•

I will giant you, you then thought, remembering something they'd once said and feeling all the better for it.
I will brighten up your eyes.

•

{*Do not forget what others have said*}

{*You will forget*}

•

{*In any event − you must*}

•

FAILURE, leading to success

through seats on the train, an eye that looked back and a face that blushed.

An arm moved past a head, pointed at a sign indicating a need for *shhh* in response to a mobile phone call and then – then it retreated.

•

You listened –
"Can't babysit these guys forever."
"It's common sense."
"Show a bit more drive."
"Make sure all the key guys are there."
"Hold on, hold on. Hold on."

•

A couple reunited at the train station on your return. He – the man – was much more excited by seeing it – the dog – than her – his wife. *Or should that be*, you thought, on watching his reaction *her – the dog – than it – his wife*.

•

In any event, she received a perfunctory kiss.

•

The night of your return you attended a party. You were asked of your ability with other languages. Someone then started –

"I can't imagine *them* being able to be so fluid with their language as we are. How can they give directions like *we* do, they're so specific?"

The English don't like to be at a loss when it comes to language, you thought of yourself, *can only function knowing all, they'll kill one of two Romanians in their company so the other is forced to speak English,* you continued, remembering something you'd once read in a book, extrapolating, aware that you were generalising, dangerously, unable to stop yourself – *and the Romanian would kill someone to eat.*

•

You started to mumble, then, after your return – so they couldn't understand you.

You no longer wanted them to.

It infuriated them.

•

"D'ya break your arm?" a fat boy asked you as you walked through London Fields the next day.

"No."

"D'ya break your arm?" he repeated.

"No."

"D'ya cut it then?"

"No."

"What then?", he shouted, completely exasperated.

•

Your appearance to him was incomprehensible.

You – well yes, of course – you sourced some pleasure in the depths of his confusion.

•

And then a woman walked toward you.

•

You didn't know her but there was an indication, however – *in the air*, you thought – that she would try to speak.
  You stopped.
  "Good afternoon", she said, and then walked on, shocking you with pleasantness. All you could say in return was a loud "thanks", even though it was not at all what you had planned to say.

•

You felt giddy afterwards.
You laughed so uncontrollably.

•

Then, thinking of the other city, walking behind someone, watching them, investigating how their black skinny jeans disappeared beneath a disappointing shirt, you felt, almost overwhelmingly, a desire to bend them over and eat their very arse.

•

{*Impossible to describe it otherwise*}

•

{*And what is it in the arse you want to eat?*}

•

You salivated, and laughed at the ridiculousness of it all, knowing that you had felt the same desire many times before, a desire that had faded as much as increased with actual deliverance of the act, an act you now found, consequently, humble.

Why do you torture yourself, or, so you then thought, being less difficult to yourself and more judgemental of others, *why is torture presented to me?*

You had no control over this return of desire, no reason nor thought could make it at all unpalatable not even that all this had happened before, had satisfied – not satisfied – had occasionally revolted.

•

You wondered why you wanted to be free of all of it.

•

On a bus into town, you noticed a man with eczematic skin.

The decision of skin not to perpetuate stereotype is most interesting, you thought.

Attractive.

•

Like Daniel Day-Lewis licks a neck in *My Beautiful Laundrette* so you then wanted it – your own – to *be licked*, you thought, or to lick that of another in return, in broad daylight, on a street, not for show, no, nor sensation, no, not as power, no, but want, yes – the dream of mutual want.

•

Sovereign Invalid

And once again you went for lunch at *Tesco*.

•

A girl sat in a wheelchair moved toward you – moved toward you in the wheelchair. You became aware of your height as you picked apples from the highest boughs of the vegetable and fruit section. You smiled down at her. You realised that she was talking to you but you could not hear what was being said. You dipped your head down, almost cradling it in her lap. You would later regret this movement, but you could not avoid it.

"Can you get lemons?"

"No problem", you said, and – before selecting – asked:

"How many do you want?"

"Doesn't matter. Just some lemons."

•

You selected two that looked much like the rest and handed them to her, delicately – only then recognising the possible inanity of your question, not least in relation to lemons.

•

Later that same week, then, consistent with return, you applied for a new job – something you had once seen advertised but disregarded as beyond abilities.

•

Surprised by the act of application, you wrote down the words *get job* on a list of *things to do* so you could immediately after writing faintly scratch them through, the order almost – but only almost – then completed.

•

And over that same weekend a woman walked the busy streets of Dalston.

•

She looked afresh for cleaning work in *Oxfam*, for which she'd been consistently refused.

Then, on Monday, ignored by all as ill, resigned to her condition, she stopped you by a shop and asked "are you all right?", to which question the answer given was – untruthfully, yes, you knew, but you could not avoid the lie – "Oh certainly, certainly. Oh indeed yes."

•

And then, you saw someone sitting on the top deck of the 74 bus, and once more you fell in love.

You were unhappy to realise that – perhaps – you still believed in it.

•

It was not the sound of the French accent that caused you to fall in love with them.

It was not even the way they had tied up their hair nor the brown skin of their small neck that such action had revealed. No and nor was it the sight of leather jacket that they now wore, a personal favorite of yours when seen on flesh of others.

No, it was the way that they had placed their foot on the headrest of the empty seat in front of them while you had looked away. That gesture – the loucheness of it, the fact that you were on a public bus, that they were still speaking on a phone, the fact that you had been thinking about the attractiveness of people as a subject of art whilst looking out the window, and somehow disregarding it – made you consider them anew, made you stop and have regard. They later looked around at you with a face and eyes that didn't interest, after they had finished with their phone call, but it didn't really matter.

You were thinking only of their foot on empty headrest, of them having just done that.

•

Their attitude prompted what you could think of only as love –
   1. temporary fascination for some material presence,
   2. disjunction concerning the normal arrangement of all things,
   3. confusion in the presence of some matter.

•

But then you looked down at your hand and at your stump. You were bleeding from what – yes – could have been a thumb. You had been picking at it throughout.

> {*Can't you recall some really good advice? Don't ever pick!*}

You had bled onto a new, cream suede jacket.
  You kept picking at it, though – and still the bus moved on.

•

Care for each body as if it were a dying language, you then thought – *and you a new born linguist.*

•

And yet – in spite of this new scope for one-eyed love – there was some awful tightness in your shoulder.

•

Your posture wasn't right, you realised – could not perhaps be made just right – especially not when sat in front of screen. Such things – and tax and rent and bodies – compelled you to constantly click and smooth your finger or your hand around a table or a pad in search of something new.

Static or moving images – it didn't really matter.

The existence of other people, the knowledge that they were there.

You looked around and found them all – completely recognisable.

You felt a rising panic at this tightness – you thought *I'm likely to collapse*.

•

They had wanted to be wanted, you then remembered once again – to be held and loved and touched.

You, in turn, had only wanted to test love, to take stump and place it down on cheek, on cheek of other, to insert it into mouth and watch them then suck hard, see them do it with some real considered pleasure.

You had wanted them to post all this on *Twitter*.

•

But neither you – nor they – could act.

•

You remembered how you took, instead, your unreformed right hand and placed it on their cheek – then traced your thumb along their bottom lip.

•

Sovereign Invalid

Just stop.

•

But why are you…

•

Sovereign Invalid

Stop.

•

"Property in London, mate – it's as good as gold."

•

Why are you trying to...

•

"Unmissable deals on all you can eat data, mate."

•

Sovereign Invalid

Can you not face this?

•

"Our best will bring out your best."

•

Oh yeah, you remembered – *got paid today, didn't I?*
  Can splash out at the supermarket.

•

Might just buy myself a tasty ready meal.

•

Sovereign Invalid

And so you ate again – then walked alone to Hackney.

•

You stood outside the Town Hall.

•

A van adorned with *Coke* livery arrived.

A car adorned with *Samsung* livery arrived as well, just seconds after.

•

Employees trailed out of both vehicles and handed out branded tambourines and blue inflatables. They could not give them out to children directly, however, who clamoured around the car and van. Parents lined up to ask representatives if they could have one – at which point they were handed over, freely.

•

You considered staying on to watch the passing of the Olympic torch.

•

You considered going to watch *The Dark Knight Rises* at the *Hackney Picturehouse* and thus avoid the procession.

You decided to watch the film, the serious work of Christopher Nolan, but Bruce Wayne – *Batman* – well, he could not die then, at the end.

He escaped the detonation of a nuclear bomb.

•

Oh Batman, you thought, just prior to leaving – *my always strong, always abiding Batman!*

•

You left the cinema – all logos and all children had disappeared.
The torch?
It had proceeded in your absence.
The athletes?
Paralympians.

•

You neither saw nor ever heard from them again.

•

So you walked by the Thames later that day and imagined thinking something, something else – *rivers,* you imagined you thought, *rivers are where the land has turned soft, where water has been permitted, by some other type of matter, to just flow.*

"If this is pleasurable, then please think it as yourself", you said out loud.

From such weakness... you continued to think.

•

{ *This thought continues*}

•

And on the journey back through London a man on train held phone.

"Yeah."

"Yeah."

"But Eric."

"Eric."

"Yeah."

•

Put phone down.
Put head in hands.

•

Sighed.

•

6.

You saw, then, some weeks later, Jill.

She talked of having *just now* met her flatmate.

•

She repeated a story, told by flatmate, how, she, flatmate, met a boy, felt a moment, a magnetism, thought he had sensed it too but... *oh, guess what*: nothing happened.

She, flatmate, returned to flat and woke to see that he, boy, had posted on his *Facebook* page a certain song.

She'd thought − *if someone posts this song on Facebook after such a night, it must mean something.*

•

Jill asked you, "Do you think so? Do you think posting a song after all that means something?"

And all you could think was − *maybe.*

You realised that you didn't know and − more so − that you didn't want to know if posting such a song on *Facebook* after one night out meant anything, at all.

But she, Jill, she wanted now to know.

She wanted to be told, in some particular way.

•

And what was it you then remembered, from that film *Alexander*, the one that got such bad reviews, that line that someone said to Irish actor Colin Farrell − *those who love too much lose everything, and those who love with irony...well, they last.*

•

But this flatmate is the same girl, Jill told you, who, in response to Jill saying she had visited her parents with her boyfriend of four months, had said, *oh no, I could never have just done that, I could never take a boyfriend home, what if he didn't like it?*

•

How could I ever take him there?

•

Sovereign Invalid

And so you thought, then, again – and this time of the other city.

•

Alan Cunningham

You thought of how whilst there you'd read some fragments of a text that you had written in a book – having read them first time 'round within another.

> {*They always end up questioning: why do you withdraw from touch?*}

•

You'd read some fragments of a text while you had visited that city, the other city that they, too, must once have also visited.

> {*They question why you…*}

You'd lain in the bed of another and had ruminated – *ruminated!* – upon a stack of books that you'd constructed by the bed, thinking: *how to write about the body – how to write of anything, at all.*

> {*You refuse…*}

•

One day you'd read:
  "everybody is humiliated from birth. The message: your very existence is a disaster, your body is a sin."
  and
  "everyone's dire, demonic, corporeality."

•

Ha Ha!

You thought of how you'd gone, then, to see someone, much later that same day – someone you had befriended since first being in that place.

•

You had sat outside their office.

•

You had sat on the pavement of the street onto which their office window looked. You'd drunk coffee and gossiped. A passerby had then stopped and started to talk to you about the various objects displayed in the window of the office – books that had been published, a half-finished wooden model of the Eiffel Tower, logo stained bookmarks.

"He is the man…" you had started to say, pointing, in response to the foreigner's English, in response to his mistake, but before you could finish what you had wanted – had thought – to say – "you want to talk to" – he had already interjected:

"And you are the woman?"

"Yes," you'd said, without much thought, "I am the very woman."

"I don't think so", he'd said, looking fiercely at your body and then back toward your friend.

•

His inquiry soon descended into the most awful vitriol.
The variety of things he hated are not worth mentioning here.

•

You had thought, then, again, again and much much further – as he'd lambasted you – about the many cities of your life.

•

You had, sadly, as example – so you then believed – only just inured yourself to the London streets where the middle classes lived, the miserably quiet terraces, counterpoint to their opposite, the chaotic angry roads. And also to the intoxicating advertisements of the major supermarkets and clothing stores, the promises offered by design and typography, the promise of empowerment, ubiquity of choice.

•

In another city, to continue, the aisles of *Lidl*, the familiar marks displayed there – the limitation of the attraction of choice – had once relaxed your shoulders and brought you almost – yes – to tears.

•

Ignoring such delights you now reopened your computer, then chose to slowly browse – although for what you weren't quite sure.

•

Whilst on the Internet an advertisement for *Waitrose* appeared from somewhere.

It featured Heston Blumenthal – celebrity, and chef.

He listed a number of ingredients that were used in the food products he'd made for the supermarket – *pop it in the oven or the microwave*, he said – from which you could later remember only one: *chilli butter*.

•

The same night as this advert had appeared you later attended a talk where a poet chose to read – you were looking for some assistance. The bit before he read the poem, however, the bit before he breathed in and started that new cadence, when he spoke with his own clumsy local voice – that's the bit you listened to.

The moment he started reading the poem – you stopped your constant listening.

•

{*No more assistance*}

•

And the next day, you went back to a *Lidl* placed in London, tried to recapture an ecstasy you had felt some years before and also to buy some razors, but whilst walking around you couldn't find anything you thought was now worth really eating.

•

As to this, however – you cried no tears.

•

You looked further on the Internet for distraction, though – the *iPlayer*, the on-demand – you read newspapers online, articles that had been written in cities and countries that you had lived in previously.

You were relieved when reading of familiar places to have memories of those places that were instead quite disappointing, not like the ones you had while lying in the bath or sitting on the bus.

•

You looked, of course, at porn.

•

But there are no cafés in London anymore, you cried out as you sat down at your desk one dark, cold fruitful night, no chip shops – *without cod who wants deep fried fish anymore?* – no, nor veterinary or medical centres administered with efficacy or with care.

•

There were only shops that sold money, traded it for watches,

{ *Recognisable brands* }

gold,

{ *Oh delicate gold* }

and silver.

•

{ *Oh wondrous, finite silver* }

•

And on the street the next day each one hailed a London bus as if it were their own – you also.

•

A woman tried to remove – no, she did remove – the cup a man had placed between his teeth so he could easily zip his jacket up. She took it out with a speed that indicated disapproval, just after you had admired his ingenuity, mirroring your own.

•

There were photographs of trees in offices to make them appear more habitable.

> { *There were in fact both real and fake-real trees* }

There was someone sitting on a bus, emanating raw sexuality.
   He was *having*, you read on the device of some strange other, what he considered to be *a most ridiculous day*.
   Perhaps it's time to get a fancy sandwich now.

•

Maybe also some brand-new running shoes, at Selfridges.

•

Did they yes, in fact, want someone young to date, someone much younger than they now were, someone who wanted to be their friend but who was cute and who they found out from the Frenchman was only 18, and they 28? Did they want someone stupid or did they want their equal? And what flaws would they accept, physical or otherwise? And those *running shoes…*

•

And lest you ever forget it – what you or they would do or not, for money or, for what is more, warm bread.

•

7.

And then?

You got an e-mail and received a phone call, both of which requested your return to good old Ireland.

A birthday party and an invitation to read at an exhibition of Irish artists.

You did not have time to go but, anyway: you went.

•

You left London by train.

You got the ferry from Holyhead to Dublin.

The train from Dublin to Dundalk.

•

Arrived at house of parents.

•

In this house, you –
 tried to open tuna tin, hoisted up your leg, laughed, placed
knee against worktop,
 laughed
 somehow attached tin opener to tin, laughed,
 turned the handle around and 'round the tin, then
 laughed
 and laughed.

•

Sovereign Invalid

Furthermore you –
   picked up phone, removed all vowels from an e-mail sister later
sent,
   sat down in the company of some other, laughed,
   laughed,
   tried to pull down jumper arm inside your coat while rubbing
it against your leg,
   laughed.

·

In addition you –

visited father/mother, laughed and they laughed too, watched, with father,

friend at kitchen sink, lift leg up, fart, noisily, say

"it's working better since I got it fixed, isn't it", at which point you had said to mother,

"what was fixed?",

then realised,

then laughed.

•

The next day –

"Jesus" you had wanted to shout, your inflection hopefully implying – *what?* – you had not been, no, wait, you *had* yes been expecting things to be quite bad but not even you had ever anticipated – such worrying decay.

How worrying? And how decayed?

Immensely, you thought – having no way then of thinking at all otherwise.

•

With that, and then just having made it, the bus took off towards Belfast.

•

3 hours later, you journeyed from Belfast to Derry by the same means – via the beauty of the Glenshane Pass.

{*Not to be described here*}

•

{*Not to be expected, being somehow* Northern Ireland}

•

On the bus you thought about what had just happened, after looking into her mouth and down your mother's throat, examining her teeth – even though you were not a dentist – informing your father that you thought he should go swimming to address his back pain, worrying about theirs, not worrying about your own, thinking, all the while, *I'm here, I'm here.*

{*I'm here*}

The loss of each tooth, for example, felt as if a little taste of death. *Anyway*, you had said – *I'm really here.*

•

You thought then about someone you had met in that other city, someone whose mother had died five years previous to your meeting, whose father had left much earlier than that. Their aunt had brought them up, they'd told you. Someone will always fill some gap – love, or hate, whichever is appropriate. What matters it to you? Decisions can be made in opposition to some earlier ones.

•

"What are your teeth like?", your mother had said to your father as he had entered the living room, as he had leaned against the radiator with some kind of aged ease.

"Oh, rotten", he had said, laughing, and then, though still caring, you had laughed too.

•

You travelled on to Derry.

•

Sovereign Invalid

You walked the city walls, sat in bars, talked to people, all with
great confidence and no lack of understanding.
Thence to Donegal.
  Arrived in Donegal town in van driven from Derry.
  Admired beautiful scenery from window of van.
  Walked to hostel on outskirts of town with friend.
  Appreciated natural beauty on walk to hostel.
  Were shown your double room.

•

Retired.

•

The next day, you woke to the sight of no friend in the room that you were sharing. You walked into town to get some breakfast – walked back to the hostel with a cup of coffee.

You saw them then, outside – and talking quietly to the owner.

"Half mad", she said, nodding at them.

"No they're ok," you thought you helpfully interjected.

"I'll cut your heads off for yes, yes", they then said and you rethought your reply – then realised they were talking only of some flowers within the garden, a polite and considered response to some work that she, owner – in passing – had mentioned needed doing.

•

And in Donegal you later left the confines of that small town, ventured further into the country, arrived at the house of another friend, where you had a vision.

You saw men writhing and fucking, you imagined it as another might see it, or as you now saw it, as you would imagine it – men, writhing, fucking and fucked in the landscaped gardens of Donegal, mouths agape in ecstasy.

You extended the scene to include all bungalows in the immediate vicinity.

In each garden men were still fucking each other – writhing, mouths agape in ecstasy.

A barbeque, set up to celebrate some forthcoming nuptials, continued, as it was.

It was only a vision in your mind, you realised, as you saw the men as they were, bare chested, drinking, perhaps one day to be replicated within a story...

•

The talk at the exhibition was not worth noting – not then, nor even, sadly, now.

•

8.

You returned to London, therefore, Ireland having proved too much for your imagination – but this you were content with.

•

And there is the strange pleasure of the correct diagnosis, you thought, *when symptoms are found to match an up 'till then imagined ailment and you have found your closest, dearest friend.*

•

"But are you English?" a man enquired of you while you were on the train, the train progressing back to mammoth London.

Without an answer he continued talking.

"You're not Polish or…you speak English? Let me tell you, been on this train, on the go, since 11.30 this morning. Not a crackhead or nothing. Here…you Irish?"

He needed something – you nodded.

"Bet you…how long you been over in England for? Bet you been here a year, go to some great university or college, don't you? I'm not trying to be funny but I'm trying to steer clear of the man looking for the tickets. Trying to be honest with you, the God's good honest truth."

You smiled.

"Here, do you have any euro on you? No they don't use euro over here, any pounds?"

You gave him one.

"Don't be offended now, I'm gonna spit on this, three times."

He did so.

"You're from Belfast, aren't ye? Been in Belfast myself, in Beechhill, Beechmount. And in Sligo and in Galway."

You didn't have the heart to tell him…

"Do you know there's a place in London you can sleep for 3 months, run by the nuns, if you're completely off the drink."

•

And at that point, then – he stopped.

•

And the threat of going back on it is needed, you thought, *before they'll let you through the gate.*

•

You were glad to be back in London, then, as the train pulled in to Euston, as you thought instead of the usual things, whatever they might be – glad, rather, that it was possible to get there, and from there to other places.

•

On the way back home from the train station, you had a new idea, however – for a brand new play.

•

You saw some men in old suits, for example, whence formerly in uniforms, laughing at a cabaret, mocking their diminished fortunes, taking pleasure in and comparing the results of intelligence tests created by now unseen captors, telling lies about books they had once read because the interrogators had laughed at their initial responses – *no*.

•

Failed suicide attempts.

•

Surprise at the continued existence of a group they had tried, desperately, to destroy.

Somebody, somewhere... well, they had really messed things up.

•

In Hackney the next day a girl asked you – whilst pointing at a sugar pot –

"Can I have some of your sugar?"

You looked at her and found the courage to say – "No."

She laughed at you and lifted it – with certainty, regardless.

You laughed at this.

You laughed together, heartily.

•

You were glad she understood exactly what it was you'd meant.

•

As a result of which you relaxed, more generally, and went to the dentist for a series of useful treatments – root canal, new crowns, etcetera, etcetera. You were surprised by the overall weakness of your teeth. You had always thought them absolutely strong. Eventually, the roots severed, the crowns fitted, the other works achieved, you quietly rose to leave.

"That tooth is now non-vital!", the dentist shouted out and after you.

•

You touched it with your tongue and, well… it felt all right to you.

•

So you phoned your mother late that same day evening, told her of your experience, tried to persuade her to spend some money and to buy the work she'd always wanted done.

"I will, I will", she said, now laughing, but you could tell by her old laugh that no, she probably never would.

•

Something in you envied her – but yet you hoped above all else she felt the stupid same; the same as you.

•

And then, later, thinking less about death and more about them, thinking again about that other city, something without definition pulled at you, pulled you away from the warm comfort of your arm around a familiar waist – it made you turn and edge away from known contact, regretting it but aware of being driven by some insatiable, indefinable need to…

•

What was it about them – about another?

•

It wasn't an exterior beauty, it was an interior aspect projected outwards by way of movement and words, *good though* had once become *good doughhh* and they had laughed, for example, as you had stuffed your mouth with just baked cookies, as they considered scope for Irish accent.

It had been an aspect of their presence that had drawn you closer, had made you desirous and careful, concerned about their allergies and sensitivities, wondrous of how they had survived within the world.

•

"I like you", you'd said, so very often.
  You'd hardly ever known them.

•

"You're only human", they had always – though very pleasantly – replied.

•

You forgot, again, about fidelity.

•

They had eaten, once, a burger from a pile that had been laid out at an art gallery and that had impressed you 'though it later pained their stomach. Thoughts of the familiar left your mind. You knew they weren't the answer but – they were an answer.

{*And yet – how many answers did you need?*}

•

You had once been entranced, you further remembered as you walked the city late one lovely night, by a mutual concern for – yes, indeed – the state of teeth, the ease with which you had spoken about such mundane matters, the way in which you had then advised – someone – to turn on their electric toothbrush as they had used it to brush their own, before you had slept with each other, not for the second time.

At a picnic after you had first met you recalled that they had asked – to no one in particular – *does anybody here know any disabled people?*

•

You had made a note to remember that, but you had not – not as of yet – made a reply.

•

And they had once suggested, to continue with examples, that you meet and make dessert together, and you had agreed, not immediately aware of what it was you were consenting to. The point being, for them, it was no major commitment. It shouldn't have been for you either, but thinking about it later...

But it was not even mentioned.

They had come, chopped the pears – as you requested – as if they'd known what it was that they would have to do. After you had cracked the cork, you still managed to open the wine, surprised that you could do it without incident.

And it was not even mentioned.

•

You hoped it never would be.

•

The next day you missed the opposite, however: a familiar presence, understanding of all your weaknesses – reverential of them, in fact, and capable of almost anything in truth.

·

No, no

{*I'm sorry, sorry*}

– the next day it was only a homeless man who was stood there, by your right side.

•

"Can I ask you a question?", he said – "You got enough money for a cuppa tea?"

"Yeah."

You reached to get some money from your bag.

"What's that? You gotta bad arm?"

"Yeah."

"Can I see it? Can I see?"

You lifted it up – your coat had kind of hidden it.

"Can I touch? Can I touch it?"

"Yeah", you said – and then you quickly closed your eyes.

•

"It's beautiful. Blessings on you."

You gave him the pound. You wanted to give him more but you had no more pounds to give.

"Did you lose it or was it like that from your birth?"

"From birth", you said.

"Gotta use the elbow, the elbow, for the punch", he said, laughing, and you, yes, *you* – you found that you were somehow laughing too.

•

The bus arrived.

"I've gotta go and get this", you said.

"Alright", he replied, shouting after you as you left, "heart of gold, heart of gold. The elbow, the elbow!"

•

And on the bus – or no, before all that, while walking to the shelter? No matter now – you remembered you had heard –

"You got some money for a cuppa tea?"

"No. I don't give out my money."

"What's that? You don't give out your money? Why? Why not?"

"I don't give out my money. I'll buy you a cup of tea."

"You'll buy me a cup of tea? You'll buy me a cup of tea? Will you buy me a sandwich? A ham sandwich?"

"I *could* buy you a cup of tea."

"Ah, you *could*. You could – but yes, you won't. How'd you have gold hair, gold hair, but not a heart of gold? Heart of silver, you have. A heart of silver. Not at all any kind of heart of gold."

•

Shut up man, you're in fucking England, someone then shouted, distracting your remembrance, as you got off the bus, as a man crossed a street in London, as you walked by, a man talking quietly on his phone but in a language they could not – you now imagined – understand.

•

{*What bothered them so?*}

{*Why not pass by in perfumed silence?*}

•

And someone later asked of you –

  "Why are you opening that packet of crackers so forcefully?"

  "I can do no other", you replied, continuing – with all your teeth – to rip at plastic.

  {*You really couldn't*}

  •

They cried when you reminded them of this, *pitying themself* you thought – 'though for what exactly you – but also they, you then assumed – well, you – or they – would never really know.

  •

That night, then, you sat down at your desk and turned on your devices once again.

•

You prioritised hand over lack and then, however, deciding to use the lack, could work neither phone – touch screens not being made for stumps – nor mouse, icons reflecting only the precision of the sole, directed finger.

The dissatisfaction of not having a finger to offer precision to your movements, to hover exactly over the *Twitter* icon, the delay it took to get that normally instantaneous reaction from your devices led to a desire to start to cry.

•

> {*This being a desire, that, once enacted, was immediately satisfying – but later, with some reflection, oh, much less so*}

•

And the next morning, you started to inspect your phone the way a mother might her child, looking for strange blemishes.

Something then distracted you, it was your...it was the end of what once could have been your thumb.

You realised then that the end of your thumb – what once could have been a thumb – was instead accumulated flesh, unrecognisable gristle and nail. It had collected into a protuberance, as, perhaps, the medical community would want to call it. Occasionally, it throbbed, and, when squeezed delicately – as you'd established in your youth – blood oozed from an unknown exit.

•

So you squeezed it, and it bled.

•

And then, inevitably, you retreated to another city.

•

9.

Leaving London – listening to Dutch, Flemish, French and Belgian – you felt an ease in your body as you failed to understand what was always being said – it really, really satisfied you.

•

You were content now, once again, with not quite knowing.

•

In Brussels Central Station you moved such that a woman could pass by you.

•

The woman stopped soon afterwards – turned around – and asked "where do you want to go?" so softly that you had to ask her to *repeat*.

"Midi", you replied, on understanding.

"I'm going that way – follow me."

•

You walked on, she leading, you following and nothing more was said as she led you from Arts-Loi, or Kunst Wet, toward the platform and then told you where to get off.

She'd had two scabs upon her face.

•

You remembered them, later, when you sat down on the train. Something in her eyes had made you want to lick that face and kiss her broken skin.

•

On the train from Brussels to Cologne you decided to speak English. You could not immediately remember any other form of language.

•

You went to the dining car and ordered a bottle of beer.

•

"Do you have a bottle opener?", you asked the attendant, upon receipt.

"Yes, I have a bottle opener", the attendant said, smiling, and then: did nothing.

After a moment however he stopped from this pursuit and looked intently at you.

"You do not have a bottle opener?", he then asked.

You shook your head.

"You have a problem, then, or no?", he said, opening the bottle for you and still smiling.

•

And all you could think of when you arrived in the other city was: a series of bad jokes.

•

Once reported by a friend, you remembered:

"Presidents can't have affairs these days.

When I look at Obama, he looks to me like he's a bit of a shagger, like JFK was.

But he can't have sex with anyone.

Because the moment he did it'd be all over social media, like 'I just had sex with Obama!', trending on *Twitter* and *Facebook*.

He'd need to have sex with someone who couldn't use social media – like, I don't know, a thalidomide victim – someone with no thumbs!!"

•

He had heard it at a comedy club in London.

The audience laughed, he had reported, sadly – "but of course they had", you'd said, smiling, later adding only to yourself: *for maybe they did not understand – no, no, not did not, instead maybe they do not understand that they have always had the option of quite calmly doing otherwise.*

•

Some days after your arrival you then started – as you almost always did – to think of what you'd do once you returned to London.

•

You thought about apartments and then porno once again – and so of course a gripping kind of fantasy developed.

•

You had established a real fantastic pattern in which – with *them* – you would now open the computer and watch pornography as a prelude to the sex, even – perhaps – continuing to watch it through the act, taking time to start new videos, if the one you watched concluded.

•

You were unsure of how they would, however, feel for all of this, apart from a vague expectation – in your mind though: always only in your mind – that given their often open appreciation of the many different forms – though you secretly thought they would always favour something opposite – and an as yet unacknowledged interest in watching others fuck, well look… you thought they might enjoy it in some way.

•

For you the interest was much clearer.

•

It allowed you to believe you were encountering all those seen for a first time,

> {*New creatures, untarnished*}

as you had once encountered them for a first time,

> {*New creature, untarnished*}

for, in your current state of mind, there was nothing so exciting as the thought of making an unfamiliar body familiar and – much more importantly – imagining having another body do so to your own.

•

> {*But never broken bodies*}

•

Your current state of mind:

You had changed, notably, since starting to move between these cities, a previous capability to imagine having been instead subsumed, a lack of aquisitorial interest in instant gratification and penetration having been somehow awoken in yourself.

•

Watching such films would satisfy an urge to make a conquest of new flesh.

•

It allowed you – so you thought – to expunge all your desires, to continue – what? To fuck? – to fuck and yet hurt no one or nobody. And yet you still wanted to do this in reality, even knowing all the shortfalls that existed between the imagined, and the real, and the consequence of confusing these great two. Your desire to do these things for real was, in fact, made even greater by the thought of some true knowledge of such things, knowing that for you – you were convinced – it would be just something close to sex, a physical act, a transaction, purchase, pleasure – and sadly nothing more.

•

Now depressed, you thought of how it had all become, once again, and with the waning of a previous, more long-term depression, a thrusting act of domination and attempt at executing some power and powerful release, leading only to sleep and a gentle, pleasurable vibration of the flesh.

•

What would any of them think of all this? Did you care? You often thought they felt the exact opposite. They enjoyed making the familiar unfamiliar – and so, for example, *you*. In the end, you had then thought, with too much imagination once again, it's *much the same thing*, the same fantasy, with always only different types of methods, different moods.

•

A fantasy of being able to satisfy, constantly, the most distant and unclear of memories – that which one thinks is a true urge.

•

The true thing maybe being this:

   What broken bodies would make you think of purchase of a body? What purchase do you think you really need? What muck, cracked bone, flesh – aging – mouth – stinking – eyes – old – the sight of which you fear – would stimulate desire?

   What repeated act?

•

What watched?

•

But you continued to be pornographic – nothing at all so safe as sex, no – you continued to desire to sell – you continued to desire to sell – things, ideas, stories – and hence to own, to have owned, to buy, ecstatically to sit, alone in cities with all your things, *computer, phone, apartment, shoes*, looking at them, carefully, considered, thinking of all those jobs there back in London, thinking of what you could yet finally earn excluding all the others, but it was all ideas, hard to implement, impossible to avoid, all in the head, ignoring the body, you cannot want the brain, in body, to disregard the body.

•

Sovereign Invalid

Fuck me from behind – you then remembered they'd once said.

{*True intimacy is not…*}

You can do what you like to me, you then remembered they'd once said.

{*True intimacy is not…*}

{*…is not without some kind of sight*}

Turn off the lights, you had said.

{*Nor laughter*}

{*There was laughter*}

•

Touch me, you had asked, still somewhat frightened by it all.

•

{*There was touch*}

•

You turned off your computer.

•

You'd spent another hour online, looking just at pictures. You had wanted to see images of them online, images of them, still, moving, it didn't really matter.
Images to quell your real desire.

•

You missed...something about them and about yourself. You tried to remember...something about them and about yourself.
   They don't like to be seen waking up, you thought, during that slow, mumbling period when the face was fresh but the owner thought it dull.

•

You almost didn't care, though, anymore.

•

You lifted up your phone and then you messaged them – told them of your worries.

"It's all within your head", they replied, almost instantly.

"Don't worry. It's in mine too", they added.

•

And an image of a smiling face then quickly followed.

•

Printed in Great Britain
by Amazon